W9-AZC-611

BALDER THE BRAVE

Writer: STAN LEE
Penciler: JACK KIRBY

Inker: VINCE COLLETTA
Colorist: MATT MILLA
Letterers: ART SIMEK & SAM ROSEN

Cover Artists: OLIVIER COIPEL, MARK MORALES & LAURA MARTIN

Collection Editors: MARK D. BEAZLEY & CORY LEVINE
Assistant Editors: ALEX STARBUCK & NELSON RIBEIRO
Editor, Special Projects: JENNIFER GRÜNWALD
Senior Editor, Special Projects: JEFF YOUNGQUIST
SVP of Print & Digital Publishing Sales: DAVID GABRIEL
Research: JEPH YORK & DANA PERKINS
Select Art Reconstruction: TOM ZIUKO
Production: JERRON QUALITY COLOR & JOE FRONTIRRE
Book Designer: SPRING HOTELING

Editor In Chief: AXEL ALONSO
Chief Creative Officer: JOE QUESADA
Publisher: DAN BUCKLEY
Executive Producer: ALAN FINE

SPECIAL THANKS TO RALPH MACCHIO

Visit us at www.abdopublishing.com

Reinforced library bound editions published in 2014 by Spotlight, a division of the ABDO Group, PO Box 398166, Minneapolis, MN 55439. Spotlight produces high-quality reinforced library bound editions for schools and libraries. Published by agreement with Marvel Characters, Inc.

Printed in the United States of America, North Mankato, Minnesota.
042013
092013
This book contains at least 10% recycled material.

Library of Congress Cataloging-in-Publication Data

Lee, Stan.
Balder the brave / story by Stan Lee ; art by Jack Kirby.
pages cm. -- (Thor, tales of Asgard)
"Marvel."
Summary: An adaptation, in graphic novel form, of comic books revealing the adventures of the Norse Gods and Thor before he came to Earth, featuring the godling Thor's attempts to prove himself to his father, Odin.
ISBN 978-1-61479-169-0 (alk. paper)
1. Thor (Norse deity)--Juvenile fiction. 2. Graphic novels. [1. Graphic novels. 2. Thor (Norse deity)--Fiction. 3. Mythology, Norse--Fiction.] I. Kirby, Jack, illustrator. II. Title.
PZ7.7.L4515Bal 2013
741.5'973--dc23

2013005291

All Spotlight books are reinforced library bindings and manufactured in the United States of America.

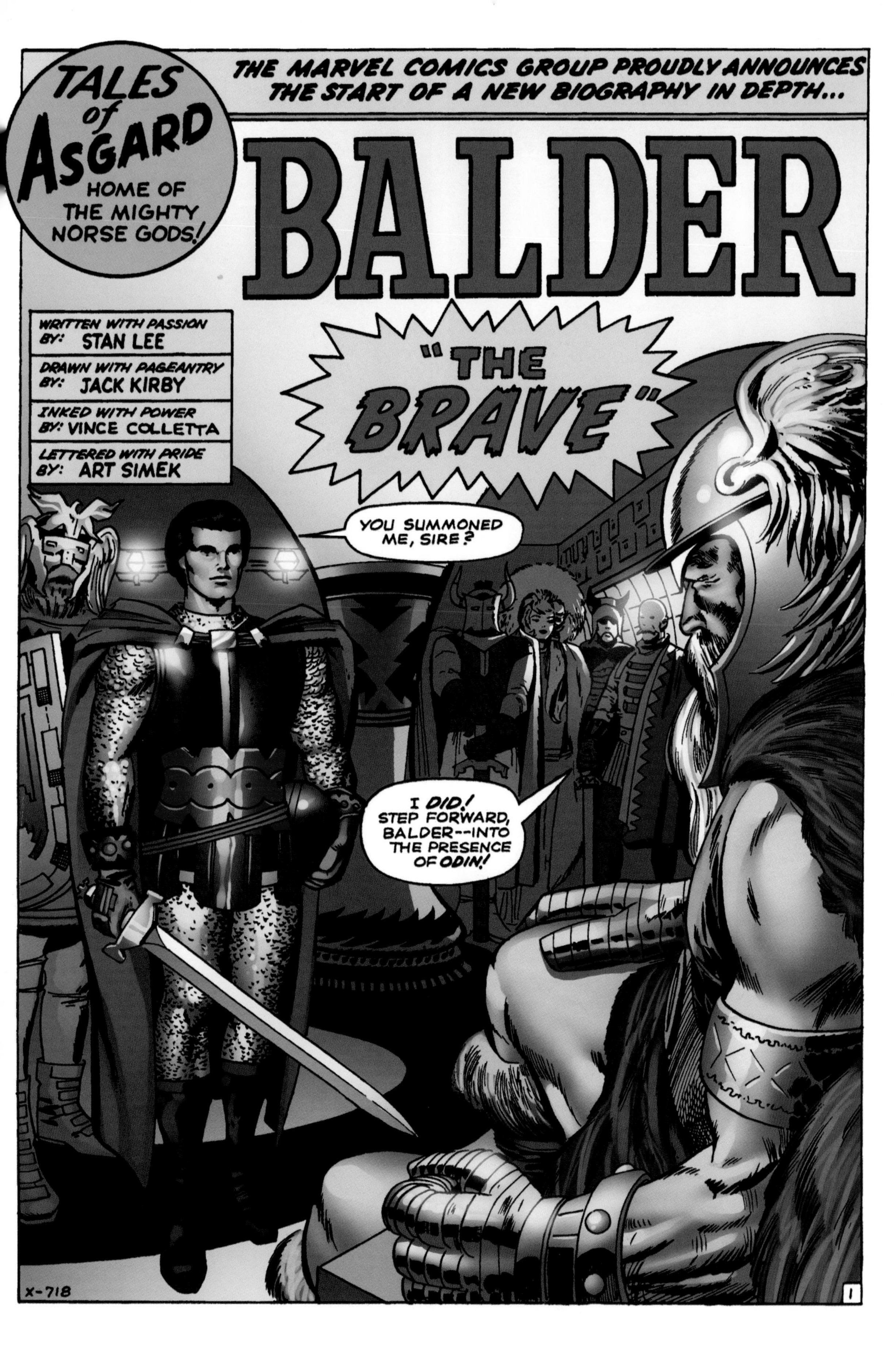
TALES of ASGARD
HOME OF THE MIGHTY NORSE GODS!
THE MARVEL COMICS GROUP PROUDLY ANNOUNCES THE START OF A NEW BIOGRAPHY IN DEPTH...
BALDER
"THE BRAVE"
WRITTEN WITH PASSION BY: STAN LEE
DRAWN WITH PAGEANTRY BY: JACK KIRBY
INKED WITH POWER BY: VINCE COLLETTA
LETTERED WITH PRIDE BY: ART SIMEK
YOU SUMMONED ME, SIRE?
I DID! STEP FORWARD, BALDER--INTO THE PRESENCE OF ODIN!
X-718
1

YESTERDAY, DURING THE FINAL BATTLE BETWEEN MY WARRIORS AND THE DEADLY STORM GIANTS, YOU DESERTED THE FIGHT WHEN WE PURSUED THEM BACK TO THEIR LAND! HAVE YOU AN EXPLANATION FOR ME, BALDER?
YES, SIRE! I SAW A BIRD FALL FROM ITS NEST, AND I TURNED TO PLACE IT BACK WITH ITS MOTHER!

WHAT??! YOU DARE GIVE ODIN SO LAME AN EXCUSE?!! FOR THAT, YOU SHALL FACE THE TEST OF MORTAL DEATH!
NO, SIRE! HAVE MERCY! BALDER'S COURAGE HAS BEEN PROVED A THOUSAND-FOLD! WE BESEECH THEE--!!
STAY YOUR TONGUES, MY FRIENDS! I HAVE NO CHOICE BUT TO DO AS ODIN COMMANDS!

MY LORD-- HEAR OUR PETITION! WE BEG THEE NOT TO SLAY BRAVE BALDER!
TAKE THE LIFE OF ONE OF US INSTEAD!
SILENCE! ODIN HAS SPOKEN! MY LAW MAY NOT BE DEFIED-- BY GODLING, OR MORTAL!

AS FAMED FOR HIS TERRIBLE ANGER AND SWIFT PUNISHMENT, AS HIS INSCRUTIBLE WISDOM, MIGHTY ODIN HAS BALDER BROUGHT TO THE AREA OF EXECUTION...
I STAND READY TO ACCEPT WHATEVER MY LORD ODIN DECREES!
2

I CANNOT BEAR TO WATCH THIS SIGHT! FOR TRULY, BRAVE BALDER IS THE MOST BELOVED OF ALL THE GODLINGS OF ASGARD!
SOUND THE TRUMPETS! LET THE SENTENCE BE CARRIED OUT!
AS YOU COMMAND, SIRE!

WITH A GRIEVING HEART, THE STEADY-ARMED TYR, MASTER ARCHER OF ASGARD, PREPARES TO CARRY OUT THE AWESOME COMMAND OF ODIN!
ONLY THE IMPERIAL COMMAND OF ODIN HIMSELF COULD MAKE ME DO THIS TRAGIC THING!

BUT, AT THE EXACT SPLIT-SECOND THAT TYR RELEASES HIS FATAL ARROW, A SHARP-EYED HAWK SWOOPS DOWN FROM THE CLOUDLESS SKY, AND...

...SEIZES THE SPEEDING ARROW IN ITS POWERFUL TALONS--MERE INCHES SHORT OF ITS UNFLINCHING TARGET!!
BRAVE BALDER HAS BEEN SAVED!!!
EVEN THE DEADLY HAWK, THAT MERCILESS BIRD OF PREY, FELT LOVE IN ITS HEART FOR NOBLE BALDER!
3

BUT THE ORDEAL OF BALDER IS NOT YET ENDED!! AT A COMMAND FROM ODIN, HIS BROTHER HONIR, CHAMPION SPEAR THROWER OF ASGARD, PICKS UP HIS TRUEST SHAFT...
I COMMAND THEE, HONIR!! LET YOUR WEAPON FLY STRAIGHT AND TRUE!!
I CAN DO NAUGHT BUT OBEY THE SOVEREIGN WE SERVE!

THIS IS A BLACK DAY FOR ASGARD!! NOW BALDER IS TRULY DOOMED!!

BUT AGAIN A SEEMING MIRACLE OCCURS! BEFORE THE HURTLING WEAPON CAN FIND ITS MARK, A STRONG-LIMBED PLANT SHOOTS UP FROM THE GROUND IN FRONT OF THE IMMOBILE GODLING!

THE SPEAR CANNOT REACH ITS TARGET!
ONCE AGAIN BRAVE BALDER IS SAVED!!!
4

THOR, MY NOBLE SON-- SYMBOL OF ALL THAT'S BEST AMONG MAN AND GODLING--GRASP THY HAMMER!!
I CANNOT DISOBEY THEE, MY FATHER! BUT IN MY HEART I PRAY FOR ANOTHER MIRACLE TO SAVE THE COURAGEOUS BALDER!

THEN, AS THE STEEL-SINEWED ARM OF MIGHTY THOR RAISES HIS INVINCIBLE HAMMER--AND AS BALDER STANDS FIRM--NEITHER FALTERING NOR FLINCHING-- THE HAND OF ODIN REACHES OUT...
ENOUGH!! THE TEST IS ENDED!! STEP FORWARD, BALDER! STEP FORWARD AND HEED THE WORDS OF ODIN...!

IT WAS I WHO SUMMONED THE HAWK --I WHO CALLED FORTH THE PLANT! FOR I HAVE A GIFT FOR THEE, BRAVE BALDER--THE GIFT OF INVINCIBILITY! THE GIFT WHICH CAN ONLY BE WON THRU TRIAL AND TEST! FROM THIS DAY HENCE, NOTHING CAN HARM THEE!
ALL HAIL TO ODIN, WISEST OF THE WISE!
HAIL TO BALDER THE BRAVE!
5

NOW FOR AGES TO COME, THE BELOVED BALDER WILL BE LIVING PROOF THAT THE BRAVEST ARE THE GENTLEST! LET GODLING AND HUMAN ALIKE NEVER FORGET THAT THERE IS ONE WHO IS INVINCIBLE--AND YET, FOR ALL HIS POWER, HIS HEART FEELS LOVE FOR THE HUMBLEST AND THE WEAKEST OF CREATURES!
THIS DAY MOST OF ALL, MY FATHER, I AM PROUD TO BE THE SON OF NOBLE ODIN!
NEXT ISSUE... PREPARE YOURSELF FOR A NEVER-TO-BE FORGOTTEN EXPERIENCE AS WE TAKE YOU ON A STARTLING JOURNEY TO-- THE LAND OF THE TROLLS!!!

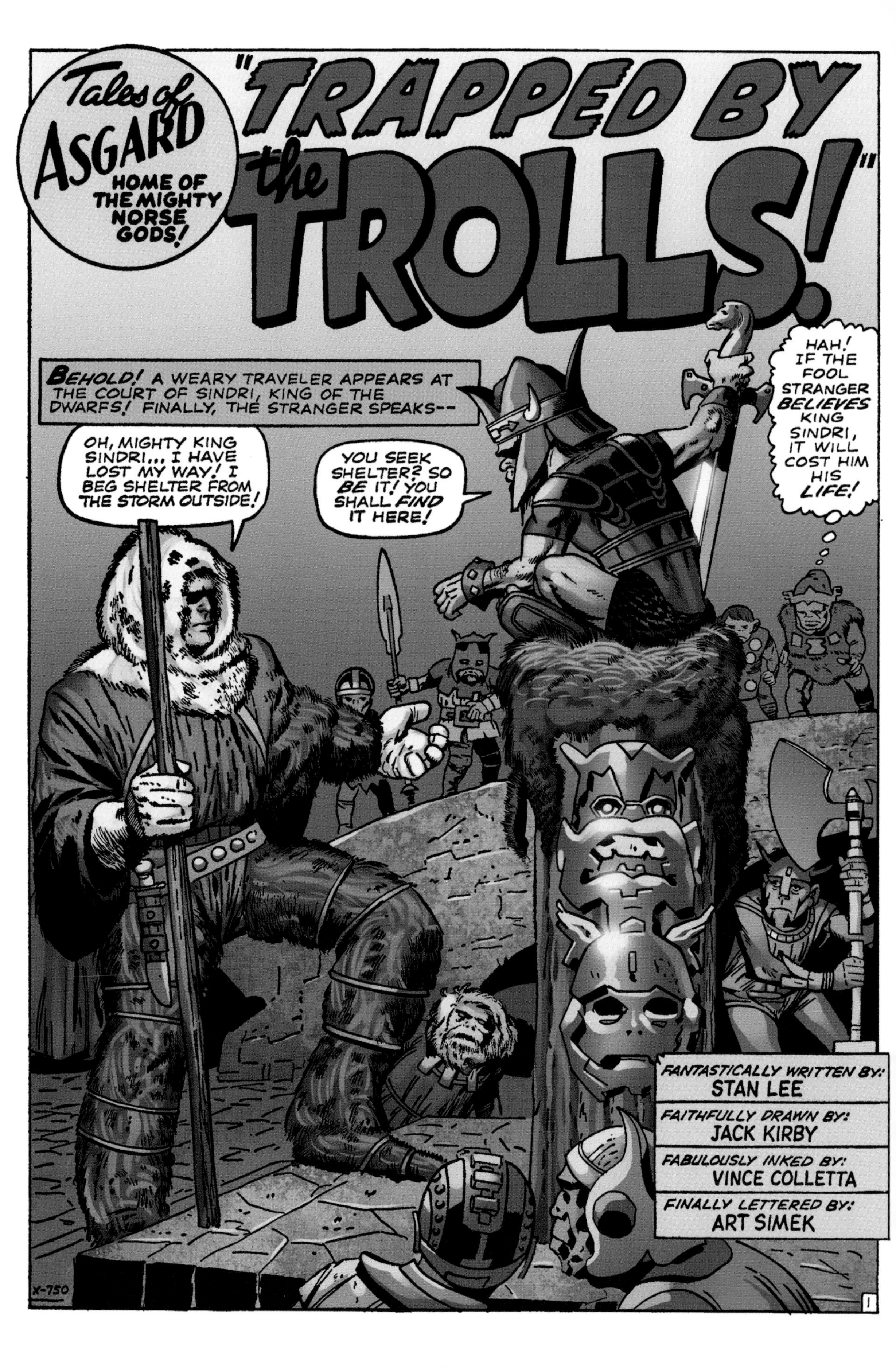
Tales of ASGARD HOME OF THE MIGHTY NORSE GODS!
"TRAPPED BY the TROLLS!"
BEHOLD! A WEARY TRAVELER APPEARS AT THE COURT OF SINDRI, KING OF THE DWARFS! FINALLY, THE STRANGER SPEAKS--
OH, MIGHTY KING SINDRI... I HAVE LOST MY WAY! I BEG SHELTER FROM THE STORM OUTSIDE!
YOU SEEK SHELTER? SO BE IT! YOU SHALL FIND IT HERE!
HAH! IF THE FOOL STRANGER BELIEVES KING SINDRI, IT WILL COST HIM HIS LIFE!
FANTASTICALLY WRITTEN BY: STAN LEE
FAITHFULLY DRAWN BY: JACK KIRBY
FABULOUSLY INKED BY: VINCE COLLETTA
FINALLY LETTERED BY: ART SIMEK
X-750
1

THE UNSUSPECTING STRANGER HAS ARRIVED AT THE RIGHT TIME! I PROMISED TO SEND ANOTHER SLAVE TO THE TROLLS TODAY--AS PART OF THE PRICE I PAY TO KEEP THEM FROM ATTACKING MY KINGDOM!

SUDDENLY, A TRAP-DOOR OPENS BENEATH THE STRANGER'S FEET, AND...
I'VE BEEN TRICKED! I'M FALLING!

GO, WITLESS TRAVELER! PLUNGE DOWNWARD-- TO THE LAND OF THE TROLLS--WHOM YOU WILL SERVE FOREVER-MORE!

HAH! HERE IS THE HOSTAGE SINDRI PROMISED US!
HE SEEMS STRONG AND WELL-FORMED! HE WILL MAKE A GOOD LABORER FOR US!
2

DISDAINFULLY, THE SAVAGE TROLLS CARRY THEIR MOTIONLESS CAPTIVE DEEP INTO THE INTERIOR OF THEIR UNDERGROUND KINGDOM, THRU WINDING CAVERNS AND TWISTING TUNNELS, UNTIL...
TO THE *WAITING CHAMBER* WITH HIM!

...REACHING A DARK, MURKY CHAMBER, THEY CHAIN THE HAPLESS PRISONER TO THE WALL, AS HE NOTICES ANOTHER CAPTIVE FROM ASGARD CHAINED NEARBY...
MY HEART IS HEAVY AT THE SIGHT OF ANOTHER WHOM THE EVIL TROLLS HAVE CAPTURED!

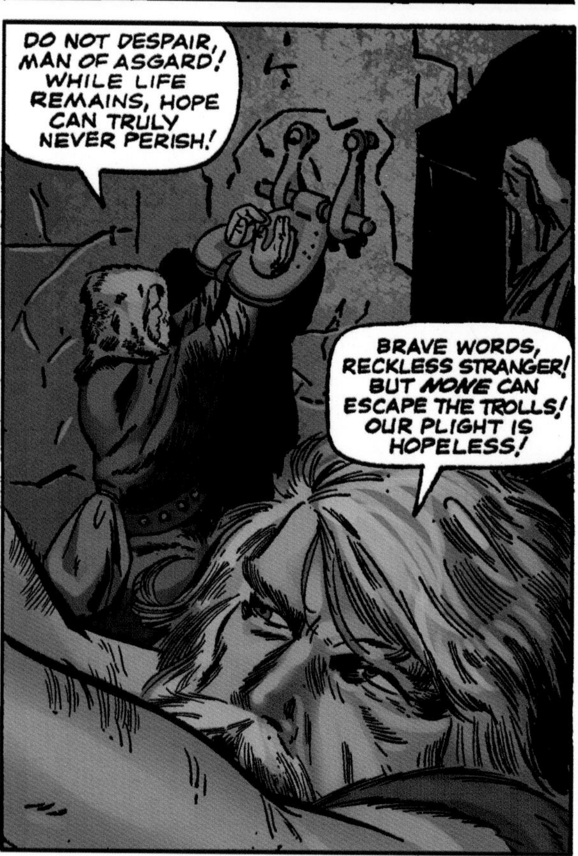
DO NOT DESPAIR, MAN OF ASGARD! WHILE LIFE REMAINS, HOPE CAN TRULY NEVER PERISH!
BRAVE WORDS, RECKLESS STRANGER! BUT *NONE* CAN ESCAPE THE TROLLS! OUR PLIGHT IS HOPELESS!

BUT--WHAT IS *THAT??* YOU HAVE LOOSED THAT SACK WHICH YOU CARRIED --AND AS IT STRIKES THE FLOOR, I SEE A *HAMMER* CONTAINED WITHIN!
3

MEANWHILE, A SHORT DISTANCE AWAY, THE CRUEL TROLL OVERSEERS DEMAND MORE AND MORE LABOR FROM THEIR HELPLESS SERFS...
FASTER, MEN OF ASGARD! WORK, OR PERISH! NONE CAN SAVE YOU ONCE YOU HAVE FALLEN VICTIM TO THE TROLLS!

YOU LIE, WICKED ONE! THEIR MOMENT OF RESCUE IS HERE! NOW YOU SHALL PAY FOR YOUR HEARTLESS OPPRESSION! BY ASGARD, HOW YOU SHALL PAY!
IT IS THOR-- THE YOUNG THUNDER GOD!
HE FREED HIMSELF BY THE POWER OF HIS HAMMER! NEVER HAVE I SEEN SUCH MIGHT-- SUCH MAJESTY! NOTHING THAT LIVES CAN DEFY THE SON OF NOBLE ODIN!

AS IF TO PUNCTUATE THOSE DRAMATIC WORDS, THOR SWINGS HIS MIGHTY MALLET BUT ONCE, AND THE VERY HEAVENS SEEM TO POUR FORTH A SURGE OF NAKED FORCE SUCH AS NO LIVING EYES HAVE EVER WITNESSED BEFORE!
4

THEN, A SECOND SWING OF THE AWESOME HAMMER CAUSES THE VERY AIR TO VIBRATE WITH SUCH UNIMAGINABLE ENERGY THAT THE PRISONERS' CHAINS ARE SHATTERED INTO NOTHINGNESS!
NOW ATTACK, MEN OF ASGARD! SHOW THE EVIL TROLLS HOW FREE MEN FIGHT! FOR VENGEANCE SHALL BE OURS THIS DAY!

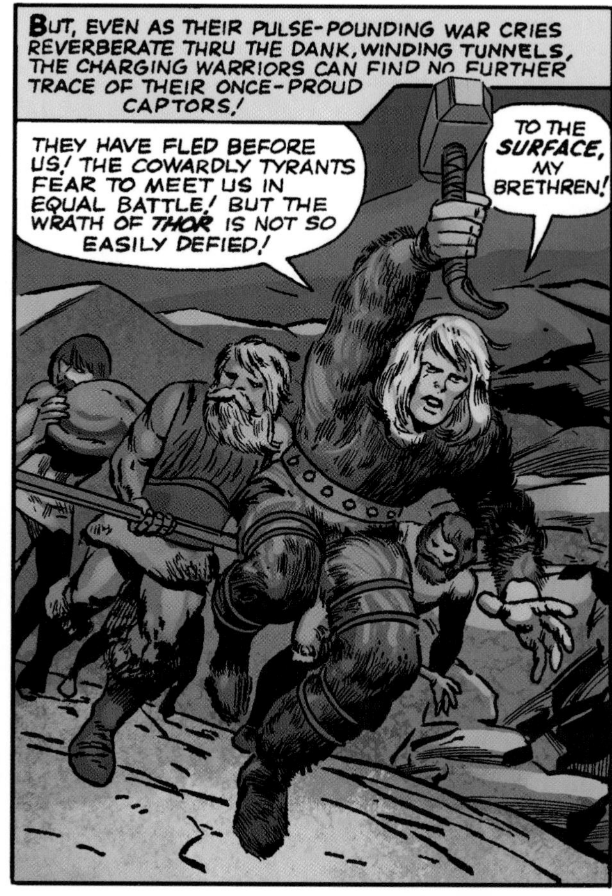
BUT, EVEN AS THEIR PULSE-POUNDING WAR CRIES REVERBERATE THRU THE DANK, WINDING TUNNELS, THE CHARGING WARRIORS CAN FIND NO FURTHER TRACE OF THEIR ONCE-PROUD CAPTORS!
THEY HAVE FLED BEFORE US! THE COWARDLY TYRANTS FEAR TO MEET US IN EQUAL BATTLE! BUT THE WRATH OF THOR IS NOT SO EASILY DEFIED!
TO THE SURFACE, MY BRETHREN!

RETURN NOW TO YOUR HOMES AND YOUR LOVED ONES! I STILL HAVE ONE MORE TASK TO PERFORM!
WE WERE FOOLS TO ABANDON HOPE! WE SHOULD HAVE KNOWN THAT ODIN WOULD NOT FORSAKE US! WE SHOULD HAVE KNOWN THAT HE WOULD SEND MIGHTY THOR TO SET US FREE!
5

LATER, AFTER ALL HAVE DEPARTED, ONE LONE FIGURE STANDS ATOP THE ENTRANCE TO THE TROLL KINGDOM, AND WITH ONE LAST BLOW OF HIS ENCHANTED HAMMER, SEALS THE OPENING FOREVER!
NEVERMORE SHALL MEN MAKE SLAVES OF OTHERS! NOT IN ASGARD--NOT ON EARTH--NOT ANY PLACE WHERE THE HAMMER OF THOR CAN BE SWUNG--OR WHERE MEN OF GOOD FAITH HOLD FREEDOM DEAR!
THE END
ANOTHER MIGHTY EPIC OF DRAMA AND DARING NEXT ISSUE AS THOR HIMSELF IS BANISHED FROM ASGARD! DON'T DARE MISS IT--YOU KNOW HOW SENSITIVE STAN AND JACK ARE!

TALES OF ASGARD HOME OF THE MIGHTY NORSE GODS!
FOR DARING TO FIGHT A DUEL AGAINST MY WISHES, YOU MUST ACCEPT MY PUNISHMENT! EVEN THE SON OF ODIN MAY NOT DISOBEY AN IMPERIAL COM-MAND! AND SO I ORDER YOU TO BE...
"BANISHED FROM ASGARD!"
The TIME: YEARS AGO, WHEN THOR WAS NOT YET 20! The PLACE: ASGARD!
PRESENTED BY THE GREATEST NAMES IN ILLO-DRAMATICS:
STAN LEE, Author
JACK KIRBY, Illustrator
VINCE COLLETTA, Delineator
SAM ROSEN, Letterer
LIVING PROOF OF THE TITANIC TALENT WHICH HAS MADE THIS SERIES SUCH A SMASHING SUCCESS!
Another MIGHTY MARVEL Saga of Epic Adventure and Powerful Pageantry!
X-781

SIRE! WE BEG YOU TO RECONSIDER YOUR VERDICT!
AT A TIME LIKE THIS, WHEN THE MOUNTAIN GIANTS ARE AT WAR WITH ASGARD, WE NEED THE MIGHTY HAMMER OF THOR!
SILENCE! JUSTICE IS JUSTICE! I WILL HEAR NO MORE!

BUT, EVEN SO HALLOWED A PLACE AS ASGARD IS NOT WITHOUT ITS TRAITORS! ONE SUCH CONSCIENCE-LESS CREATURE IS... ARKIN, THE WEAK, COUSIN OF EVIL LOKI!
SO! THOR HAS BEEN BANISHED FROM ASGARD! THAT MEANS HE WILL HAVE TO RIDE THE MOUNTAIN ROAD ALONE!
THIS NEWS MAY SERVE TO SOFTEN THE HEART OF THE MOUNTAIN QUEEN TOWARDS ME... I MUST TELL HER WITHOUT DELAY!

LONG HAVE I LOVED KNORDA, NORMAL-SIZED QUEEN OF THE MOUNTAIN GIANTS... BUT LONG HAS SHE SPURNED MY HEART!
BUT, WHEN I BRING HER MY TIDINGS SHE WILL SEE THAT ARKIN IS NOT WEAK! PERHAPS SHE WILL FIND ME WORTHY OF HER LOVE!

AND SO, ON A DESOLATE MOUNTAIN RIDGE, JUST OUTSIDE THE FABLED LAND OF ASGARD...
THE NEWS YOU BROUGHT MAY MEAN THE DEATH KNELL OF ASGARD! DO YOU REALIZE THE EXTENT OF THE TREASON YOU HAVE COMMITTED, ARKIN??
YES, BEAUTIFUL QUEEN! BUT IT MATTERS NOT, SO LONG AS YOU LOOK WITH FAVOR UPON YOUR ADORING SLAVE!
2.

TIME ENOUGH TO DISCUSS SUCH MATTERS LATER! NOW I MUST ACT! FIRST, WE SHALL DISPOSE OF THOR... AND THEN... ALL ASGARD SHALL BE OURS!
I CARE NOT WHAT FATE BEFALLS THE SON OF ODIN... NOR THE LAND OF ASGARD! I CARE ONLY TO WIN THE HEART OF QUEEN KNORDA!

LATER, THE MIGHTIEST WARRIOR THE WORLD HAS EVER KNOWN SLOWLY RIDES ALONG THE MOUNTAIN ROAD WHICH LEADS AWAY FROM THE LAND OF HIS BIRTH...
THE TRAIL I FOLLOW IS FRAUGHT WITH DANGER... BUT AN IMMORTAL OF ASGARD MUST SHOW NO FEAR! NO MATTER WHAT BEFALLS, I AM THOR, SON OF NOBLE ODIN!

THEN, SUDDENLY, WITHOUT WARNING... THE GRAVEST DANGER OF ALL APPEARS, AS A HEAVILY-ARMED BAND OF MOUNTAIN GIANTS ATTACKS THE LONE WARRIOR IN AN AWESOME ASSAULT FROM AMBUSH!
RIDE, MY POWERFUL LEGIONS! SHOW THE BRASH YOUNG THUNDER GOD NO MERCY! ASGARD MUST BE MINE!
3.

BUT, NOT FOR NAUGHT HAS THE PROWESS AND DARING OF THOR LIVED IN LEGEND FOR ALL THESE AGES! FEARLESSLY, AS THOUGH FOLLOWED BY HIS OWN LOYAL LEGIONS... THE GOLDEN-HAIRED IMMORTAL THUNDERS THROUGH A NARROW CANYON PASS... HIS SMALLER STEED RACING LIKE THE WIND WHILE HIS LARGER PURSUERS SLOW DOWN IN ORDER TO ENTER!
YOU CANNOT ESCAPE US, PUNY ONE! THE MORE YOU FLEE, THE SWEETER WILL BE THE FRUITS OF OUR ULTIMATE VICTORY!

NOW HE IS TRULY TRAPPED! HE HAS LED US INTO A WALLED-IN VALLEY, FROM WHICH THERE CAN BE NO ESCAPE!

STOP HIM... BEFORE HE ENTERS THE MOUTH OF THAT SMALL CAVE! WE CANNOT FOLLOW IN SO LIMITED A SPACE!
BAH! IT MATTERS NOT! IF HE REMAINS WITHIN, WE SHALL STARVE HIM OUT! PANIC HAS MADE A FOOL OF THE SMALL ONE!

BUT, THE GLOATING MOUNTAIN GIANTS MIGHT NOT FEEL SO CONFIDENT IF THEY COULD LOOK WITHIN THE CAVE, AND SEE...
THIS NARROW TUNNEL IS JUST WIDE ENOUGH TO ALLOW MY STALLION AND ME TO REACH THE TOP OF THE CANYON!
4.

THUS, THE WARRIORS OF ASGARD ADD ANOTHER VICTORY TO THEIR GLORIOUS HISTORY! BUT, NEXT ISSUE, BE PREPARED FOR A SURPRISE! FOR YOU WILL READ THE NEVER-BEFORE-REVEALED ACCOUNT OF THE TIME ODIN *LOST* A CRUCIAL BATTLE... THE TIME HIS LEGIONS WERE FORCED TO ACCEPT *DEFEAT!* AND NOW, UNTIL WE MEET AGAIN, MAY THE BLESSINGS OF ASGARD BE SHOWERED UPON YOU!

Tales of ASGARD
HOME OF THE MIGHTY NORSE GODS!
the DEFEAT OF ODIN!
THE ENEMY APPROACHES, SIRE!
IN WHICH NOBLE ODIN, LORD OF ASGARD, MONARCH OF THE LEGENDARY NORSE GODS, SUFFERS HIS FIRST DEFEAT!! OR--DOES HE??
WARRIORS, ASSEMBLE! PREPARE FOR BATTLE!
ANOTHER TOWERING TRIUMPH BY MARVEL'S TALENTED TITANIC TEAM:
STAN LEE WRITER
JACK KIRBY ILLUSTRATOR
VINCE COLLETTA DELINEATOR
ART SIMEK LETTERER
1

RAMPOK THE REBEL IS DEAD!! RAMPOK, THE KING WHO HAS DARED TO DEFY THE RULE OF ODIN FOR AGES! RAMPOK, THE KING WHOSE LEGIONS HAVE LONG BEEN AT WAR WITH ASGARD! AND NOW, RAMPOK'S SON, PRINCE RIVVAK, TAKES UP THE BATTLE....!
WE SHALL ATTACK THE ARMY OF PRINCE RIVVAK HEAD ON! AT MY COMMAND, WE SHALL CHARGE ACROSS THE BOILING PLAIN!!
BUT, MOST HONORED FATHER, WHY ATTACK THEM WHERE THEY ARE STRONGEST?? WHY NOT STRIKE AT THEIR FLANK?
SILENCE!! I HAVE SPOKEN!

SEE THEM WAITING ACROSS THE BOILING PLAIN! THEY THINK I HAVE NOT THE COURAGE TO CROSS IT IN FRONTAL ASSAULT!! WELL, RIVVAK HAS MUCH TO LEARN!!

AND WHAT OF YOUNG PRINCE RIVVAK, FACING HIS FIRST BATTLE AS LEADER OF HIS LEGIONS?
OUR PRINCE IS ASHEN PALE! METHINKS HE HAS NO STOMACH FOR YON COMING BATTLE!
I AM SICK WITH FEAR AT THE THOUGHT OF FACING ODIN'S WARRIORS!! AND YET, I MUST NOT SHIRK MY DUTY!
OFFICERS! OUR TRIAL IS AT HAND!

DIRECT YOUR MEN TO STATION THEMSELVES IN BATTLE FORMATION!
METHINKS HIS VOICE SHOWS SIGNS OF FALTERING!
CAN ONE SO YOUNG-- ONE SO UNSURE --LEAD US AGAINST SO MIGHTY A FOE??
AND YET, WE HAVE NO CHOICE! WE MUST OBEY THE YOUTHFUL RIVVAK, NO MATTER WHAT THE COST!
2

AND THEN, A ROARING, EAR-SPLITTING, REVERBERATING CRY RINGS OUT FROM THE ARMY OF ASGARD AS PRINCE RIVVAK AND HIS WARRIORS PREPARE TO MEET THE MOST POWERFUL LEGIONS OF ALL TIME!
ATTACK!
FORWARD!! FOR ASGARD!!

AND, ACROSS THE VAST BOILING PLAIN...
LANCES AT THE READY!! CHARGE!

BUT, BEFORE THE TWO ARMIES CAN MEET, THE SEETHING POTHOLES BENEATH THEIR FEET SUDDENLY ERUPT, AS GIGANTIC FLAMING GEYSERS SHOOT SKYWARD!
LOOK TO YOUR STEEDS, MEN OF ASGARD!! THEY HAVE NOT BEEN TINGED WITH IMMORTALITY, AS WE HAVE! THE FLAMES MUST NOT TOUCH THEM!
3

THE FIERY GEYSERS SHOOT UPWARD WHEREVER WE RIDE --AS THOUGH THEY HAVE WILLS OF THEIR OWN!
BUT NONE APPEAR BENEATH THE ADVANCING WARRIORS OF RIVVAK!

NO WEAPONS IN THE UNIVERSE CAN TURN BACK OUR CHARGE-- BUT WE DARE NOT ENDANGER OUR VALIANT STEEDS WITH THESE BLAZING GEYSERS!!
TRUMPETER!! FOR THE FIRST TIME SINCE THE DAWN OF MAN--SOUND THE RETREAT!!

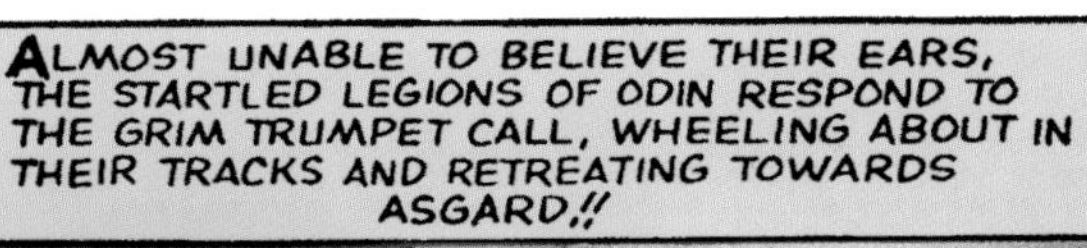
ALMOST UNABLE TO BELIEVE THEIR EARS, THE STARTLED LEGIONS OF ODIN RESPOND TO THE GRIM TRUMPET CALL, WHEELING ABOUT IN THEIR TRACKS AND RETREATING TOWARDS ASGARD!!

WHILE THE YOUNG PRINCE, FLUSHED WITH TRIUMPH, PURSUES THEM TO THE EDGE OF THE FLAMING GEYSERS!
FLEE, SOLDIERS OF ASGARD! EVEN NATURE CONSPIRES AGAINST YOU!!
NEVER AGAIN SHALL I TREMBLE WITH FEAR BEFORE AN ENEMY! FOR NOW I KNOW THAT NO ONE IS UN-BEATABLE! THERE IS NO BATTLE THAT CANNOT BE WON!
4

AND SO WE LEARN THAT THERE ARE *MANY* WAYS TO WIN A VICTORY--MANY WAYS TO ACHIEVE A GOAL! IN THE CASE OF ODIN, LORD OF ASGARD, HIS GOAL WAS HELPING MANKIND, AND ONLY THE TRULY STRONG, ONLY THE TRULY COURAGEOUS, WILL DARE TO *LOSE* A BATTLE--IN ORDER TO GAIN A TRIUMPH! NOW, UNTIL OUR NEXT EPIC OF ASGARD, MAY THE WISDOM OF ODIN BE SHOWERED UPON THEE!

ODIN

Real Name: Odin
Occupation: Lord of Asgard
Identity: Publicly known to the citizens of Asgard, regarded by the citizens of Earth as mere myth
Legal status: Citizen of Asgard
Other current aliases: All-Father
Former aliases: Woden, Wotan, Atum-Re
Place of birth: Unknown
Marital status: Married
Known relatives: Frigga (wife), Thor (son), Loki (adopted son)
Group affiliation: Gods of Asgard
Base of operations: Dimension of Asgard
First appearance: JOURNEY INTO MYSTERY #85

Origin: Odin was born ages ago as a member of the race of gods who would one day be called Asgardians. Although the precise circumstances of his birth are lost in antiquity, Odin is believed to be the son of Buri, one of the first great Asgardians, and Bestla, a frost giantess. Odin's parents produced two other sons as well, Vili and Ve. The three brothers eventually assumed leadership of the fledgling tribe of gods and helped them establish themselves in the dimension now known as Asgard. As ages passed and the gods rose and fell and rose again stronger than before, Odin gradually achieved ascendancy within the tribe. Finally at the twilight of the last age, it was Odin who mystically redistributed the Asgardians' life-forces into their current physical incarnations. Having done so, Odin was given the name All-Father, and has ruled Asgard as its absolute sovereign ever since. Though he took Frigga as his wife, Odin chose to mate with the non-Asgardian Earth-goddess Gaea (whom he knew as Jord) to produce a son who would have qualities beyond those of any Asgardian. This son was named Thor.

In recent years, Odin sacrificed his right eye to Mimir the All-Knowing Well of Wisdom in order to learn how to thwart Ragnarok, the cyclic cataclysm that brings a fiery end to the age. With the help of his son Thor, Odin managed to avert the natural coming of Ragnarok, perhaps indefinitely. Odin is attended by two mystical ravens, Hugin and Munin (whose names mean "Thought" and "Memory," respectively), who help him to survey the realm. Odin dwells in his royal palace at the center of Asgard's capital city, but also has a palace in Valhalla, overlooking the Land of the Honored Dead.

Height: 6' 9" **Weight:** 650 lbs
Eyes: Blue **Hair:** White

Powers: Odin possesses the conventional physical attributes of an Asgardian male ("god"), as well as the greatest single share of power in all Asgard. Like all Asgardians, he is extremely long-lived (though not immortal in the same sense as the Olympians), superhumanly strong (the average Asgardian male can lift about 30 tons; Odin can lift 60), is immune to all diseases, and resistant to conventional injury. (Asgardian flesh and bone is about 3 time as dense as similar human tissue, contributing to the Asgardians' superhuman strength and weight.) His Asgardian metabolism gives him far greater than human endurance at all physical activities.

Odin possesses vast energy powers of an unknown nature. Magical in their apparent form and function, these powers can be employed for numerous purposes, among which are: the augmentation of physical strength and endurance, the enchantment of beings or objects, and the projection of energy bolts. Odin's enchantments (such as the one he placed on Thor's hammer, Mjolnir, to return to the thrower's hand) last until he rescinds them or they are overpowered by a superior enchantment. Odin can also create interdimensional apertures with a gesture and project a 3-dimensional, audio-visual image of his visage, visible to only those he wishes, across space or dimensions. Odin commands the life energies of the entire race of Asgardians, and can absorb any or all of their life energies into his person at will, or in certain instances, restore life to an Asgardian whose life energies are ebbing. (He cannot resurrect the dead once they have passed into the dominion of Hela the Death Goddess.

At periodical intervals, approximately once every Earth year, Odin is required to sleep for about a week to renew his godly energies. If Odin misses the "Odinsleep," or is awakened before it is through, his power level begins to diminish. (Once while in such a state, his power diminished to the point that he could be drugged and kidnapped by aliens.) Odin's power is also dependent upon the dimension of Asgard itself. Unlike his son Thor, Odin's power wanes when he is on Earth or another dimension.

Odin is not omniscient, nor can he create life from nothingness, travel through time unaided, read thoughts, teleport (except interdimensionally), or move worlds. He is, however, perhaps the most powerful mythological god still active today.

Weapons: Odin wields the trident Gungnir (the "spear of heaven") and the power scepter Thrudstok, a small mace. Both of these weapons are made of uru metal and are objects through which he can channel his power. He also wears Draupnir (the "Odinring") as a symbol of supremacy. The specific properties of the ring are yet unknown.

Transportation: Odin rides the eight-legged steed Sleipnir, who can fly through the air at incalculable speeds. He sometimes employs Skipbladnir, a Viking longboat whose enchanted sails and oars enable it to navigate the "sea of space." Skipbladnir can be mystically shrunk to the size of a fist.

TALES OF ASGARD #1 (1968) COVER BY JACK KIRBY & MATT MILLA

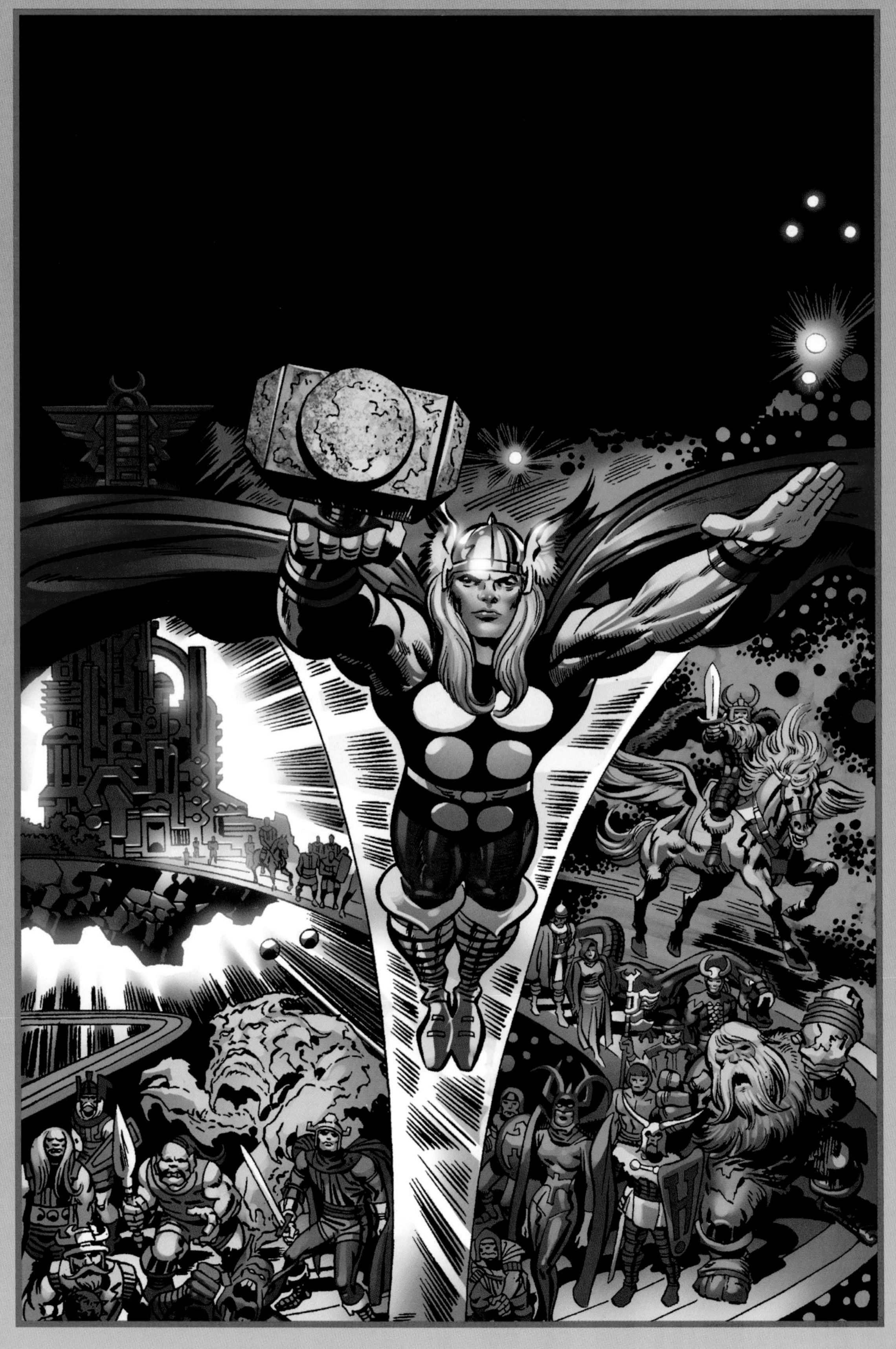